Illustrated

THERE'S A HIPPOPOTAMUS UNDER MY BED

By Mike Thaler

AN AVON CAMELOT BOOK

2nd grade reading level has been determined by using the Fry Readability Scale.

AVON BOOKS
A division of
The Hearst Corporation
1350 Avenue of the Americas
New York, New York 10019

Text copyright © 1977 by Mike Thaler
Illustrations © 1977 by Ray Cruz
Published by arrangement with Franklin Watts, Inc.
Library of Congress Catalog Card Number: 77-23457
ISBN: 0-380-40238-6

First Avon Camelot Printing: October 1978

CAMELOT TRADEMARK REG. U.S. PAT. OFF. AND IN OTHER COUNTRIES, MARCA REGISTRADA, HECHO EN U.S.A.

Printed in the U.S.A.

BAN   20   19   18   17   16   15   14

One day a hippopotamus followed
me home from school.

He sat down in my father's best chair.

He looked like my uncle,
so I named him Morris.

Then I gave him a bath.

He liked it.

I dried him well.

And I tied a ribbon around him.

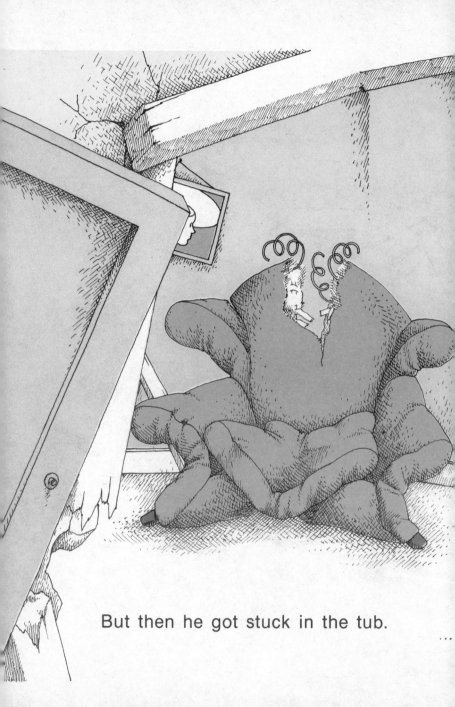

But then he got stuck in the tub.

"What a mess! I'd better
hide you, Morris, before
Mother and Dad come home."

So I hid him in with the coats.

It didn't work.

I tried to disguise him.

That didn't
work either.

Then I had an idea.

"Something is odd here,"
said Dad.

"Junior, what's been going on here?"

"Nothing. Let's have dinner.
I bet you're hungry.
I set the table."

"Oh, what a good boy."

"Junior, what's this?"

"He's Morris. He's my hippopotamus, Dad.
He followed me home from school."

"Can we keep him? He could sleep
under my bed."

"And Mother could use him
as a trash can."

"And he would chase away robbers.
PLEASE!"

"Can we keep him?
Can we keep him?"

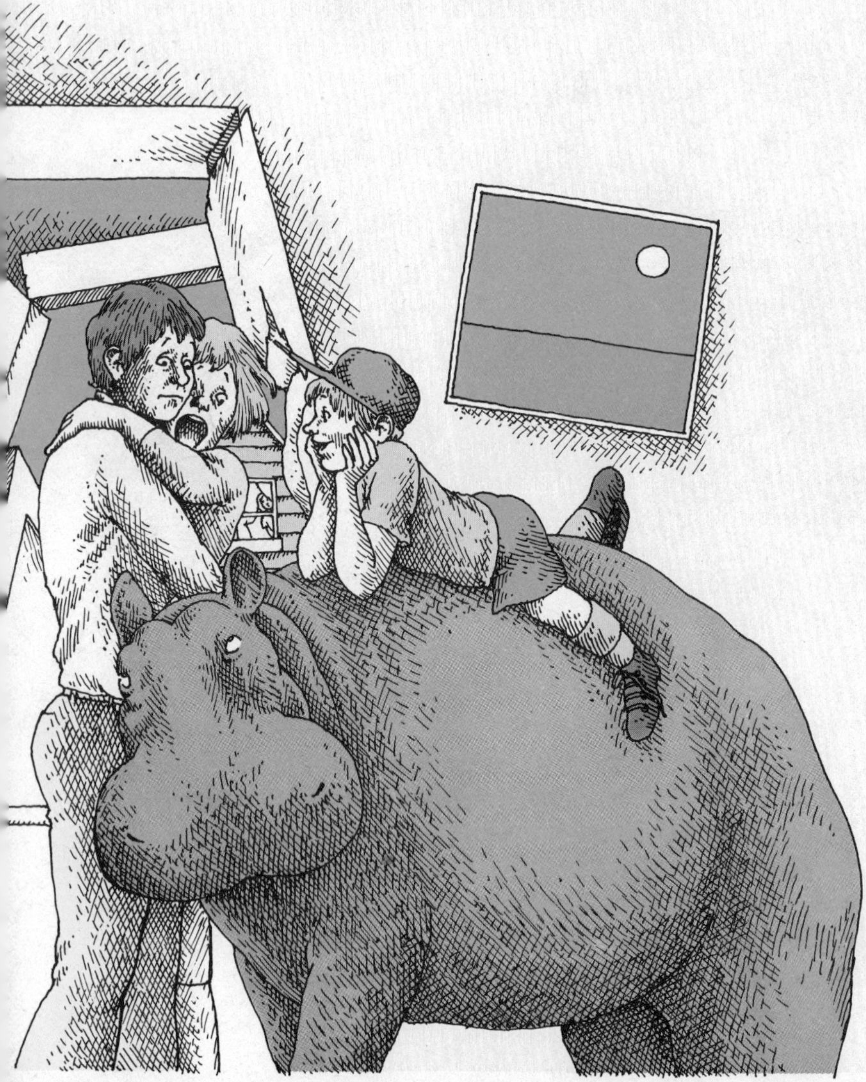

Knock, knock, knock.
"We're from the zoo.
Have you seen a hippopotamus
about this wide?"

Well, they took Morris back
to the zoo. They gave him
a new ribbon and a new bathtub.
But I'm the only one who
can give him a bath.
And I do, everyday after school.
He likes it.